**Put Beginning Readers on the Right Track with
ALL ABOARD READING™**

The All Aboard Reading series is especially for beginning readers.
Written by noted authors and illustrated in full color, these are books
that children really and truly *want* to read—books to excite their
imagination, tickle their funny bone, expand their interests, and
support their feelings. With three different reading levels, All Aboard
Reading lets you choose which books are most appropriate for your
children and their growing abilities.

Level 1—for Preschool through First Grade Children
Level 1 books have very few lines per page, very large type, easy
words, lots of repetition, and pictures with visual "cues" to help
children figure out the words on the page.

Level 2—for First Grade to Third Grade Children
Level 2 books are printed in slightly smaller type than Level 1 books.
The stories are more complex but there is still lots of repetition in the
text and many pictures. The sentences are quite simple and are broken
up into short lines to make reading easier.

Level 3—for Second through Third Grade Children
Level 3 books have considerably longer texts, use harder words and
more complicated sentences.

All Aboard for happy reading!

To Alison Powers — J.F.

To Timmy Martin — D.D.R.

Text copyright © 1992 by Jean Fritz. Illustrations copyright © 1992 by DyAnne DiSalvo-Ryan. All rights reserved. Published by Grosset & Dunlap, Inc., which is a member of The Putnam & Grosset Group, New York. ALL ABOARD READING is a trademark of The Putnam & Grosset Group. Published simultaneously in Canada. Printed in the U.S.A.

Library of Congress Cataloging-in-Publication Data
Fritz, Jean. George Washington's mother / by Jean Fritz ; illustrated by DyAnne DiSalvo-Ryan. p. cm.—(All aboard reading) Summary: Describes the life of the mother of our first president and her relationship with her children. 1. Washington, Mary Ball, 1708–1789—Juvenile literature.   2. Presidents—United States—Mothers—Biography—Juvenile literature. 3. Washington, George, 1732–1799—Juvenile literature. [1. Washington, Mary Ball, 1708–1789. 2. Washington, George, 1732–1799. 3. Presidents—Family.] I. DiSalvo-Ryan, DyAnne, ill. II. Title.   III. Series. E312.19.W33F75 1992 973.3′092—dc20 [B] 91-34247   CIP   AC

ISBN 0-448-40385-4 (GB)   A B C D E F G H I J
ISBN 0-448-40384-6 (pbk.)   A B C D E F G H I J

ALL
ABOARD
READING™
Level 3
Grades 2–3

George Washington's Mother

By Jean Fritz
Illustrated by DyAnne DiSalvo-Ryan

Grosset & Dunlap • New York

MARY MONTAGUE

COLONEL JOSEPH BALL

Everyone has a mother. Even George Washington. Of course, she hadn't always been his mother. Once she was just Mary Ball, a pretty girl from Virginia. Pretty as a rose. That's what people said. She had a sweet voice. And she was not poor. Her parents had died and left her some land and two horses. Also two gold rings. Furniture, plates, a tablecloth and napkins.

She was born in 1708 when Virginia was an English colony. By the time that she was twenty-one years old, Mary still wasn't married. Her friends married at sixteen. Or seventeen. Or eighteen. But not Mary. Why? Maybe no one suited her. Maybe no one asked. In any case, Mary had a mind of her own.

Then one day when she was twenty-two, along came Augustine Washington. He was tall and strong. He looked as if he could take good care of her. He was thirty-seven years old and had taken care of one wife for years. She was dead now, and he was looking for another wife. He already had two big boys. But they'd be no trouble. They were going to school in England soon.

So he asked Mary to marry him. And she said she wouldn't mind.

Mary and Augustine were married on March 17, 1731.

George was born on February 22, 1732. He didn't look special. He didn't look as if he would become the Father of his Country. All people said was that he looked like his ma.

A year later Betty arrived. She looked exactly like George. Then Samuel came. And John. And Charles.

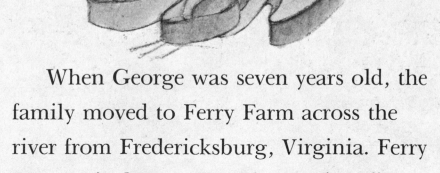

When George was seven years old, the family moved to Ferry Farm across the river from Fredericksburg, Virginia. Ferry Farm suited Mary Washington just fine.

For one thing, she loved the well. She had never tasted better drinking water. For another thing, nobody else lived nearby.

With no neighbors around, Mary would not have to dress up every afternoon. Mary hated to dress up. She could wear her old gardening clothes all day. Who would care?

If she had callers, maybe she would
dress up. Maybe she wouldn't. But of
course she would serve her gingerbread.

Everyone raved about Mary
Washington's gingerbread. She always cut
off the crusty endpiece. (This was called
the "kissing piece." No one ate that.)
Then she sliced up the rest and passed it
around. And around. And around.

These were happy years at Ferry Farm. The children were still small. She could keep track of them. She liked that. And Augustine took care of the farm.

Then in 1743 Augustine died. Of course, he couldn't help dying. But who was going to take care of things now? Augustine owned land all over Virginia. What would happen to that? Mary was not pleased with what happened. Most of the land went to Augustine's boys by his first wife. Much less went to Mary's boys.

Right away Mary began to feel poor. She had no reason to feel poor. Ferry Farm would belong to George when he was twenty-one. She and her family could

go on living there. The farm had 9 cows,
9 other cattle, 11 sheep, 19 hogs, 2 horses.
And there were 20 slaves to work the place.
She would never go hungry.

    Still, Mary grumbled and worried.
George was the man of the house now.
But he was only eleven years old.
Why shouldn't her stepsons help?
<u>They</u> had all that land. <u>They</u> were living
in style.

So Mary sent George first to August
and then to Lawrence. Lawrence was
George's favorite brother. He had fine
friends, gave fine parties, and lived in a
fine home. He called it Mount Vernon.

When George was fourteen, Mary
thought he should come back to Ferry
Farm. To stay. But George was like his
mother. He had a mind of his own. And
he wanted to go to sea. Join the navy.

Mary had never heard such foolishness. The sea was not a safe place. And how could George take care of her at sea? Lawrence begged Mary to let George go.

Mary said, "No." Lawrence argued. For one year he argued.

Mary still said, "No, no, no."

Then she said, "Maybe." She wrote to her brother, Joseph, in England. He would know what to do. He knew everything. She wrote, but she didn't hear and didn't hear.

So at last Mary gave in.

George packed his trunk and was ready
to leave. But just then a letter arrived from
Joseph. George would be crazy to go to
sea, he said. Sailors were treated like dogs.

So that was that. Mary told George to unpack his trunk. What could George do? Nothing. She was his mother. And he wasn't twenty-one years old yet.

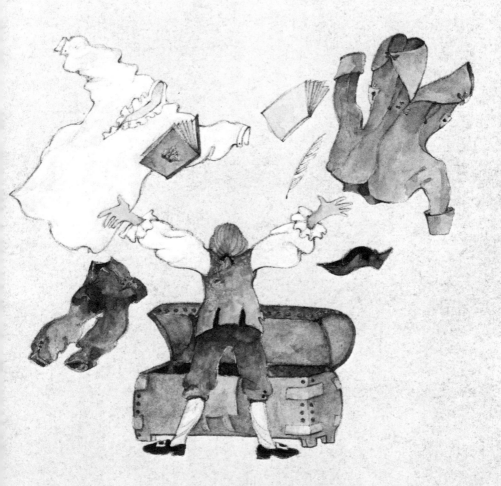

Still, Mary found it hard to keep that boy on the farm. He traveled all over with Lawrence and his friends.

In August 1752 Lawrence died. A few months later Lawrence's wife remarried and George became master of Mount Vernon. <u>Now</u> he'd surely stay put, Mary thought. He wouldn't be as close. But he could still take care of her.

Then George joined the army. He became an officer in the Virginia Volunteers. He wore a fancy uniform. He learned to use a sword. And he drilled. He didn't go anywhere. So Mary didn't mind.

VERY NICE, DEAR.

But in 1753 the governor asked George to go west to the Ohio River. The French and English were arguing about land. There might be a battle, the governor said.

This time George didn't ask his mother. He <u>was</u> twenty-one years old now. He just went. When Mary heard, she grumbled. Why was George meddling with the French? she asked. They were none of his business. <u>She</u> was his business. Suppose she ran out of money?

Right away she felt poor.

Well, George did fight. He didn't win. But he came home. Safe. At least that's what the paper said. But Mary didn't trust the paper.

Mary had to see for herself. So she went to Mount Vernon. Yes, George was safe. And thank goodness! He was through with the army.

So that was that, Mary thought. <u>Now</u> George would stay put. She asked him for some money and went home.

But that was not that. Two years later an English general arrived in Virginia. He was going after those French again. He asked George to come along.

At the last minute Mary heard about
it. She jumped on her horse and rode to
Mount Vernon.

Mary flung herself into the house. And
there was George, ready to go. Mary lit
into him. George listened. He was polite.
But she knew that look on his face. It was
his stubborn look.

What could Mary do? She was his
mother. But George was a grown man.
And he had a mind of his own. She
stamped out of the house and rode home.

George went off. And Mary tried to get along. But she ran out of things. Once she ran out of butter. And where was George? Off meddling. She wrote him a letter. Please send some butter, she said.

Butter! Here George was, about to go into battle. No one had enough food. Or water. Many of the men were sick. And his mother wanted butter!

He wrote to her. There was no butter where he was.

When the battle came, it was a bloody one. The English lost. More than half of them were killed or wounded. Two of George's horses were shot. George returned to Mount Vernon. Sick. Tired. Unhappy.

Mary wrote to him. Don't ever, <u>ever</u> go
to war again, she begged. But how could
George promise? How did he know what
would happen?

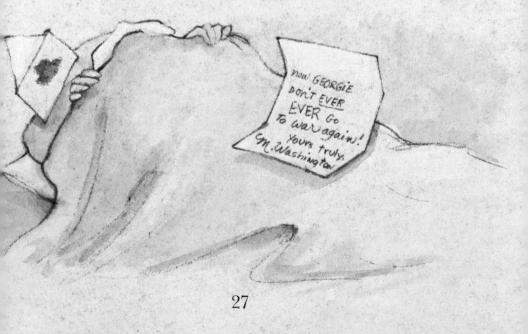

now! GEORGIE
DON'T EVER
EVER Go
to war again!
Yours truly,
M. Washington

AT LAST!

Then on January 6, 1759, George married Martha Custis. <u>Now</u> he'd stay put, Mary thought. She wrote to her brother, Joseph. There had been no end to her troubles with George, she said. All those years in the army. "But now he has given it up." Her troubles were over.

All of Mary's children were grown and moving away. Betty was married and lived in Fredericksburg. So Mary was alone on the farm. She didn't mind.

Like many country women, Mary liked to smoke a pipe. So sometimes she did. George wouldn't have approved. But George wasn't there, was he?

Of course George and Martha did come to see her. He'd look over the farm. Often it was in a mess. Mary did not run things well. George gave her money. And more money. It didn't help. She still felt poor.

Mary was sixty years old in 1768. The
farm was a lonely place to live, George
told her. She should move to Fredericksburg.
Near Betty.

Mary had never heard such foolishness. Drink Fredericksburg water? Leave her well? Dress up every day? Not on your life! George argued with his mother. But Mary would not hear of it.

Then in 1772 George bought a house in Fredericksburg for his mother. Next door to Betty. George said he would pay a man to run Ferry Farm. And this man would send Mary food from the farm. Chickens and eggs too.

Mary didn't give in right away. But suppose she did give in? Someone could bring her water from her well. She could dig up the plants from her kitchen garden. And take them with her to Fredericksburg. So Mary moved across the river.

33

She planted a garden at her new house.
Mint, sweet peas, rosemary, daisies.

She made gingerbread for the children
of the neighborhood.

And often Mary walked over to Betty's
to visit. Betty still looked exactly like
George. Sometimes the children would beg
her to imitate him. So she would put on a
cape. And a man's three-cornered hat.

She'd take her husband's sword. Then
she'd tell everyone to stand at attention.
And everyone would. They might even
salute. They had good times together.

Sometimes Mary liked to be alone. She would go behind Betty's house and sit on a large flat rock there. She loved that rock. It was her special place. She would listen to the quiet and forget her troubles. She didn't even worry about George.

But trouble was on the way. People in the colonies were fussing. What was the king of England doing to them? Taxing them. Taking away their rights. Mary didn't go along with that talk. Her brother, Joseph, was loyal to the king. So she was too.

Of course, George had to be in the middle of the fuss. Meddling again. Drilling troops in Virginia. Getting ready to fight the king. Maybe the colonies would even break away from England. Maybe they would try to rule themselves.

On April 19, 1775, Americans fought
their first battle against the English.
George was made the top general of the
army. Mary was not surprised. But the
king was not going to like that, Mary
said. She knew what would happen.
One day the king would hang George.
And right away she felt poor.

George went from battle to battle.
Mary read about him in the paper. He was
in Boston. In New York. In New Jersey.
But what did the paper know? She liked
firsthand news. But she didn't get much
news from George.

The war went on and on. And Mary felt poorer and poorer. She grumbled about hard times. She even asked neighbors for money.

Once she wrote to her son John. "I never lived so poor in my life," she said.

Once she wrote to the people in the Virginia government. She was the mother of George Washington, she said. And she was "in want." Could they give her an allowance?

George heard about this. And he put a stop to it. Fast. He wrote to the people in Virginia. His mother was not "in want." Her children would never let her be "in want."

George asked his brother John to talk to her. Her "wants" were all in her mind, George said. And endless. She must stop taking money from friends.

The war finally ended. America had won. Now it was going to rule itself. After the last battle, George went to Fredericksburg. And soon he was back at Mount Vernon. Mary was seventy-five years old now. And she was not well.

Why didn't she move in with one of her children? George asked. But not with him. She wouldn't like Mount Vernon.

He had so much company. Important
company. She would have to dress up
all the time.

Mary didn't want to move anywhere.
She would just stay put, she said.

At home Mary didn't dress up. Not even for George's important friends. Once a famous French general came to call. She had on her black cotton gardening dress. But she didn't care.

She served him a mint drink. And gingerbread. They had a nice visit.

In February 1789 George Washington was elected President of the United States. Mary was not surprised. Who else would they choose?

In August, Mary Ball Washington died. She was eighty-one years old. She was buried just where she wanted to be buried. Beside her quiet rock.

The whole country made a fuss over her. All the men in the President's house wore black badges on their hats. They tied black ribbons on their swords. They wore black bands on their arms. And there were no parties for a week.

The papers printed fancy words about Mary. She wouldn't have believed them. But they did call her "the President's mother." And she was that.